A NorCal Press Publication

The Adventures of Fin Man

By Kristin Pedderson

Description

The Adventures of Fin Man by Kristin Pedderson is an inspiring story of courage, transformation, and environmental heroism. Fin Man, a unique hero born of the sea, is half-man, half-dolphin and dedicated to a powerful mission: to save the oceans and restore balance to the world's waters.

As Fin Man teams up with mystical Guardians from diverse marine realms, he embarks on thrilling adventures to reverse pollution, protect coral reefs, and confront threats to marine life. Set against vibrant underwater landscapes and infused with a message of hope and resilience, this book is a call to action, inviting readers of all ages to become stewards of our planet.

About The Author

Kristin Pedderson is a passionate author and musician who is an advocate for positive change. Her work spans books, music, and inspirational content, all centered around themes of personal growth, resilience, and environmental stewardship.

Known for her vibrant storytelling and uplifting messages, Kristin creates works that encourage readers to explore their own journeys and connect deeply with the natural world.

The Adventures of Fin Man highlights her dedication to ocean conservation and youth empowerment.

Prologue

Long before the world knew his name, the oceans whispered of his coming. Beneath the shimmering surface of the vast seas, a destiny was being forged—one that would change the course of history and restore balance to a fragile world.

The ocean, with its mysteries and untold depths, had been both a cradle and a battleground, holding the secrets of life and death for eons. Now, it was dying.

Pollution had poisoned its waters. The once-vibrant coral reefs, teeming with life, had turned to ghostly skeletons.

Marine creatures, once free and majestic, struggled to survive in a world no longer hospitable. The oceans cried out for a savior, for someone who could bridge the gap between the world of humans and the world of the sea.

And then, he was born.

Fin Man was not like other beings. He was of two worlds—human and dolphin, land and sea.

His father, a brilliant scientist, had devoted his life to unraveling the mysteries of the sea. His mother—an extraordinary dolphin of rare grace and intelligence—saw even deeper, sensing truths hidden in the ocean's depths and in the heart of the man who loved her.

Together, they brought Fin Man into existence—a being shaped by science, spirit, and the deep's own longing for renewal. He was not merely born; he was *called*—destined to rise as a champion of the oceans and ignite a revolution of restoration.

But this was no ordinary mission. Fin Man's path would carry him to the farthest reaches of the underwater realm, into trenches where sunlight had never touched and kingdoms older than memory still breathed.

There, the ancient Guardians of the sea awaited him—keepers of forgotten wisdom, challengers of the unworthy. They would test him, temper him, and awaken the dormant powers woven into his very being.

For Fin Man's destiny was not simply to defend the ocean. It was to *heal* it.

And in the quiet pulse of the tides, in the hush between waves, one truth echoed through the deep: The oceans had chosen him.

Introduction

He was the dream of the dolphin and born of the sea. His parents were unique. His father, Buck, was head of science at the Marine Mammal Aquatic Research Park. And his mother was the loveliest of swimmers, a true friend to the father of Fin Man.

They were young when the two grew close together, the parents of Fin Man. At 18, Buck left home to join the Marines. He fell in love with the sea. His bunker studied the vast world beneath the surface while working to protect and defend the United States waterways from intruders and destructive forces.

This was in the sixties. A time when many questions would arise regarding the planet, the oceans, and the future of humanity. Much has happened since then

Lovelygirl was Fin Man's mother, a dolphin who could see deep into the gentle soul of Buck—the marine who would one day change the course of evolution.

They'd swim together daily, sharing a unique bond. Buck would hold tight to the fin of "Lovelygirl" (the dolphin's pet name), and they would traverse the coastal waters of Honduras.

Never had a human being experienced such an adventure. Buck spent all his spare time with Lovelygirl. And if he wasn't with her, he would miss her. They had a connection like no other, and he could hardly wait to see her again. Their senses were elevated when together, and the two caressed and kissed like the waves that would rise against the shore.

There was a heightened awareness whenever the two were together, as if the water itself held its breath. And one dusk, their swim was unlike any before it. Energy gathered around them, shimmering through the currents. Their hearts aligned, their bodies moved in perfect harmony—until the boundary between them dissolved, and two became one.

Not long after this time, Lovelygirl gave birth, and Fin Man was born. He was half man and half dolphin. Strong and agile with the heart of a human and the soul of the sea.

And because Fin Man's birth was so unique, there was no doubt the pair's offspring came for a special purpose.

Buck knew this and Lovelygirl understood. So, the two together did everything they could to teach Fin Man the importance of doing good in the world. They knew Fin Man was alive to save the oceans.

Table Of Contents

Chapter 1
The Birth of Fin Man

In the quiet depths of the ocean, where the sun's rays barely reach, a dream was taking form—a dream that would one day swim to the surface and change the course of history.

This dream belonged to a dolphin, a creature of the sea known for its intelligence, grace, and deep connection to the mysteries of the water. Her name was "Lovelygirl" by the humans who knew her. She was a force of nature and unlike anyone else. Playful and curious, she had a bond with a marine named Buck that defied explanation.

Buck was not an ordinary man. As a child, he had been captivated by the ocean, spending every spare moment near the water's edge. His eyes would scan the horizon for any sign of life.

His love for the sea led him to pursue a career in marine biology, and by the time he was twenty-five, he had become the head of science at the Marine Mammal Aquatic Research Park.

Buck devoted his work to studying the behavior and communication of marine mammals—especially dolphins. And it was here, in the heart of that research, that he first met Lovelygirl.

Their meeting was during one of Buck's research dives off the coast of Honduras. Buck had been swimming and diving, collecting data regarding coral formations.

On a dive, he felt something nudge him from behind. He turned around and saw Lovelygirl for the first time. Her sleek body gliding effortlessly through the water, her eyes locked with his. It was as if she could see into his very soul, understanding him in a way no human ever had.

From that moment, a dream began to take shape. Soon, Buck and Lovelygirl were inseparable. And it wasn't long before their connection grew into something far deeper than science alone could explain.

Each morning, Buck swam out to the same place—just beyond the reef, where the water ran clear, and the currents moved like a gentle breath. Lovelygirl was always there waiting for him. He would take hold of her dorsal fin, and together they glided into the deep, exploring the ocean's hidden wonders: caves glowing with phosphorescent algae, shimmering schools of fish that moved as a single living tapestry, and vast underwater forests of kelp swaying like green cathedrals in the tide.

And when they swam together, Buck felt something awakening within him. His senses sharpened; every shift in the current, every flicker of movement in the deep became clear to him in ways he couldn't explain.

His body moved with a new ease, instinctively matching the rhythm of the sea. It was as though the ocean recognized him and welcomed him. Drawing him into its ancient pulse. And little by little, it shaped him.

One day, as Buck and Lovelygirl swam through a particularly deep canyon, something extraordinary happened. A powerful current swept them into a hidden grotto, a place Buck had never seen or visited before.

The water was warmer and glowing with a strange, otherworldly light. And at the center of the grotto was a large, pulsating orb of energy, emitting waves of warmth and light that made the water shimmer like liquid gold.

Lovelygirl nudged Buck toward the orb, and as he reached out to touch it, a surge of energy shot through him. He felt his body change, his limbs becoming stronger, more fluid, and his senses expanding even further. He could hear the song of the whales from miles away, and he felt the pulse of the ocean's currents as if they were part of his own heartbeat.

It happened in an instant—sudden, undeniable—and as quickly as it began, the transformation surged through him and was finished.

Now Buck floated in the water, dazed. His mind struggled to comprehend what had just happened. Lovelygirl swam beside him, her eyes filled with a strange mix of joy and sorrow. She led him out of the grotto and back to the surface, where the sun was setting in a blaze of orange and red.

And as Buck climbed back onto his boat, he realized that something within him had changed forever. He was no longer just a man—he was something new. A man who belonged to both the land and the sea.

Months passed, and Buck continued his work at the Marine Mammal Aquatic Research Park, but he was no longer content to merely study the ocean. He wanted to protect it. And he wanted to heal the damage that humans had done to it over the centuries.

For this reason, he spent all his extra hours in the water, swimming with Lovelygirl. He always learned something new. Like the ways of the sea creatures. He even used his newfound abilities to communicate in intriguing ways with them.

He cared deeply about the ocean and did not hesitate to speak up on its behalf with his fellow Marine Mammal Aquatic Research Park employees and co-workers. He sought to defend the ocean from those who would harm it.

One day, Bucks' beloved Lovelygirl was found to be pregnant with a child. Not long after this, she gave birth.

Buck was amazed at the idea of another dolphin and calf to care for and embrace. And so he was there, swimming beside Lovelygirl as she brought her calf into the world.

But this was no ordinary dolphin calf. As the baby emerged, Buck saw that it was different—its body was more human-like, with arms and legs instead of fins; however, its skin was smooth and gray like a dolphin's.

The calf opened its eyes, and Buck saw that they were his eyes—human eyes, filled with the same curiosity and intelligence that he had always seen in Lovelygirl's gaze.

Buck understood then that this was no ordinary child. This child was the result of a bond that transcended the boundaries of species. A being born of both land and sea. And so he decided to call him Fin Man.

Fin Man was a miracle, and a creature of the ocean, with the heart of a human. Clearly, destined for a purpose greater than any that had come before.

Now, as Buck cradled the newborn in his arms, a profound sense of responsibility settled over him. He knew that Fin Man would one day face challenges unlike any the world had ever seen. There was so much they would need to learn—

about the ocean, about destiny, and about each other. And Buck understood one thing with absolute certainty: they would face it all together.

Remembering The Journey

Buck recalled the orb and the early moment when his life was changed that day, swimming with Lovelygirl months ago. He could never forget. He understood and felt that this was all a part of a Universal plan from the creator of the Universe.

He understood that Fin Man would rise in his place, stepping into the immense challenges that the future would demand.

Time went by, and as the Fin Man grew, he learned from both humans and dolphins as well as all the creatures of the sea.

He held a profound love for humanity and the creatures of the deep, and he sensed that he would one day be summoned to stand between the ocean and the forces determined to destroy it.

Buck was a very wise man who also knew that Fin Man had everything that would be required: the strength, the wisdom, and the love needed to succeed. The ocean had given him a gift, and it was now his duty to help Fin Man fulfill his destiny.

For Buck, Fin Man was a symbol of hope in a world that desperately needed it. He was the dream of the dolphin, the child of the sea, and he would grow to become a guardian of the ocean, a protector of all life beneath the waves.

His journey was just beginning, but already, the currents of fate were guiding him toward a future where he would play a crucial role in saving the ocean and with it, the world.

Chapter 2
The Call of the Deep

Fin Man grew quickly, his body and mind developing in ways that defied explanation.

By the time he was a teenager, it was clear that he was no ordinary being. His muscles were firm, powerful, and streamlined, allowing him to swim at incredible speeds. And his lungs could hold air for hours, letting him dive deeper than any human could imagine.

But it wasn't just his physical abilities that set him apart; Fin Man had an innate connection to the ocean, a sense that the sea was alive and that it was calling to him.

Buck did a proper job raising Fin Man with the love and care of a devoted father. And Fin Man had grown through changes to where Buck could clearly recognize progress in his son.

Sometimes, Fin Man would stare out into the horizon with a distant gaze. As if listening to a voice only he could hear.

When Buck asked him about it, Fin Man would simply smile and say, "The ocean is speaking to me, Dad. It wants me to come home."

The Cavern Of Conviction

One night, when the moon was full and the tides were high, Fin Man couldn't resist the call any longer. So he slipped quietly into the water, his body moving with effortless grace as he swam out into the open sea.

The farther he went, the stronger the pull became, until he found himself in the deepest part of the ocean, where the water was as black as the night sky, and the pressure was enough to crush an ordinary man. However, Fin Man was no ordinary man.

He continued to dive deeper, following the call that resonated deep within him. He kept going until he reached a place where the water glowed with an eerie light. And what was now before him was a massive underwater cavern. A place where its walls were covered in strange, bioluminescent creatures that flickered like stars.

Curiously, Fin Man swam inside, feeling a sense of awe and reverence, as he moved deeper into the cavern.

And within the heart of this cavern, Fin Man found himself in a vast, open chamber filled with a soft, pulsating light.

In the center of the chamber was a group of ancient marine spirits, their forms shifting and changing like the currents of the sea. They were the Ocean Elders. Guardians of the deep. And they had been waiting for Fin Man.

"Welcome, child of the sea," one of the Elders spoke, its voice echoing through the water like the sound of a distant whale song.

"We have been expecting you."

Fin Man bowed his head, feeling both humbled and honored to be in the presence of such powerful beings.

"Why have you called me here?" he asked, his voice steady but filled with curiosity.

The Elder's eyes glowed with ancient wisdom as it spoke.

"The ocean is in great peril, Fin Man. The balance of life that has existed for millennia is being destroyed by the actions of mankind. Pollution, overfishing, and climate change are wreaking havoc on our waters, and if nothing is done, the oceans will die."

Fin Man felt a surge of anger and sadness at the Elder's words. He had seen the signs of destruction himself—coral reefs bleached and dying, fish populations dwindling, and plastic waste floating in the currents.

"What can I do to help?" he asked, his voice filled with determination.

The Elders surrounded him, their forms swirling like a living current.

"You are unique, Fin Man," another elder spoke, with a voice gentle yet powerful.

"You are born of both the land and the sea, and you possess the strength and wisdom of both." The lead Elder went on, "You have the power to heal the oceans. You can restore the balance that has been lost. But you cannot do it alone. You must unite the Guardians of the sea with the people of the land. Only together can the oceans be saved."

Fin Man nodded, understanding the weight of the task before him.

"I will do whatever it takes," he vowed. "I will protect the ocean and all its inhabitants."

The Elders nodded with approval, their light glowing brighter.

"We will guide you," they said in unison.

"But remember, Fin Man, the path ahead will not be easy. There will be those who seek to stop you. For there are those who profit from the destruction of the seas. You must be strong, wise, and above all, compassionate. The ocean is alive, and it responds to those who love it."

With those final words, the Elders began to fade, their forms dissolving into the water. However, before they disappeared completely, they bestowed upon Fin Man a gift—a glowing pearl that pulsed with the energy of the ocean itself.

"This is the Heart of the Sea," the first Elder said.

"It contains the essence of the ocean. Its strength, and its life force. Use it wisely, for it will aid you in your journey."

Fin Man accepted the pearl, feeling its warmth in his hand. And as the last of the Elders vanished, the chamber began to darken. Fin Man knew it was time to return to the surface.

Swiftly, he glided out of the cavern.

The Heart of the Sea was glowing softly in his grip as he began his ascent. And as he broke the surface, the sun was rising, casting golden light across the water.

Now Fin Man felt a renewed sense of purpose and determination. He knew what he had to do, and he knew that the journey ahead would be filled with challenges. But he also knew that he was not alone—the ocean was with him, guiding him and giving him strength.

The Adventure Begins

As he made his way back toward the shore, Fin Man could feel the power of the Heart of the Sea resonating within him. This energy was connecting him to the very life force of the ocean.

He felt a rising excitement for whatever dangers were ahead and was ready to unite with the Guardians of the deep and the people of the land in a shared cause.

The ocean had called to him, and he had answered without hesitation. His sense of purpose and resolve was strengthened. He had been changed from the inside out.

He allowed himself a moment of rest, knowing that when dawn came, his mission would truly begin. Now it's not just an idea he carries. But a force that carries *him*.

Fin Man was ready to save the seas.

Chapter 3
Coralyth The Guardian

The sun shone brightly as Fin Man swam through the clear, turquoise waters of the Great Barrier Reef. Beneath him, the vibrant colors of the coral spread out like an underwater garden, teeming with life. Fish of every shape and hue darted between the coral branches, and sea turtles glided gracefully through the water, their ancient eyes reflecting the wisdom of the deep.

But as beautiful as the scene was, Fin Man could sense that something was terribly wrong.

The coral, once healthy and strong, was beginning to fade. Some of the branches were bleached white and brittle to the touch, and they were lifeless. The water felt warmer than it should have, and there was a stillness in the current that made Fin Man uneasy.

The reef, which had thrived for thousands of years, was dying, and with it, the countless species that depended on it for survival.

Fin Man knew he had to act quickly. The warnings of the Ocean Elders echoed in his mind—countless dangers were closing in on the seas. And among them, the devastation of the coral reefs stood as one of the most urgent and heartbreaking threats.

Without the reefs, the ocean's ecosystems would collapse, leading to the extinction of countless marine species. But he also knew that this was not a battle he could fight alone.

As he swam deeper into the reef, Fin Man focused on the Heart of the Sea, the glowing pearl that the Elders had given him. He could feel its energy pulsing in his hand, connecting him to the ocean's life force.

Closing his eyes, he reached out with his mind, calling to the ancient spirits of the reef.

"Come and meet me."

For a moment, there was only silence, and Fin Man feared that his call had gone unheard. But then, the water around him began to shimmer and swirl, and he felt a gentle, soothing presence envelope him.

Opening his eyes, he finally saw her—the Coral Guardian, Coralyth: an ethereal being woven from light and water.

She said, "I am Coralyth the Radiant,"

Coralyth is the embodiment of renewal within the reef realms. Her very presence glows. Where she moves, the water flows gently, and dormant reefs stir awake as if recognizing an old friend.

Coralyth's power is not forceful; it is restorative. She is calm and impactful, carrying the quiet authority of ecosystems that have endured for millennia. Her voice is like a distant whale-song, soothing yet commanding. Coaxing life back into places long thought lost.

Fin Man had a knowing that she is the first Guardian and one to remember every reef's first bloom and every wound it has ever suffered. She holds an unwavering belief that even the most damaged places can rise again.

Coralyths' form was shifting and flowing like living coral brought to life. She radiated a sense of hope for Fin Man.

She was beautiful and ancient as the reefs themselves. Her body shimmered with the colors of the coral: brilliant reds, blazing oranges, deep purples, and vibrant greens, shifting like living light beneath the water.

Her eyes, deep and wise, reflected the endless cycles of life and death that had played out in the ocean for millennia. And as she approached, Fin Man could feel her sadness and pain at seeing the reef in such a state.

"Why have you called me, Fin Man?" Coralyth asked, her voice a soft, melodic whisper that carried the weight of ages.

"I seek your help," Fin Man replied, his voice filled with urgency. "The coral is dying, and with it, the life of the ocean."

"The Ocean Elders have sent me to restore balance to the seas, but I cannot do it alone. I need your guidance, your wisdom, and your power to heal the reef and protect it from further harm."

Coralyth the Radiant swirled as she exchanged glances with Fin Man and the reefs.

"The reef is dying because of the actions of man," she said, her voice tinged with sorrow. "The oceans are warming, the waters are polluted, and the balance of life has been disrupted.

We have tried to protect the coral, but our power alone is not enough. Its the enormity of the matter. Humanity must change its ways if the reef is to survive."

Fin Man nodded, understanding the implications of the task before him.

"I will do everything in my power to bring that change," he vowed. "But first, we must heal the reef, so that it can continue to support the life of the ocean. We must build, harvest, and plant new coral under the sea to restore the coral reefs. Will you help me?"

Coralyth the Radiant spoke gently. "Inside every coral, small algae called zooxanthellae make life-giving energy through the power of sunlight. The coral depends on them, just as they depend on the coral's safe embrace. It is a symbiosis as ancient as the sea itself."

Fin Man replied, "Studies at the Marine Mammal Aquatic Research Park have brought hope. My father, Buck, taught me about one possible solution: Coral Trees. These trees are tethered to the ocean floor and buoyed with a subsurface float. Coral fragments are hung from the branches of the tree using monofilament line."

Fin Man continued, "Each tree can hold up to a hundred coral fragments, but they need enough space between them to grow properly." He gestured toward the swaying structures. "Suspended in the nutrient- and sunlight-rich water column, these fragments develop into healthy young colonies. In six to nine months, they'll be strong enough to outplant back onto the reef."

Then Fin Man said, "We can absolutely do this!" He continued, "Once the corals reach a healthy size, they're tagged and transported to a carefully chosen restoration site, where each fragment is secured to the reef using a two-part marine epoxy."

Coralyth the Radiant was silent for a moment, her form shifting as she contemplated all Fin Man had spoken.

After some time, she spoke again and said, "I will help and support you in these efforts, Fin Man. But know this—the healing of the reef is only the beginning. The true challenge lies in ensuring that it does not suffer again. I need you to go to the people of the land and show them the importance of this project. To protect and preserve our efforts. Only then can the balance be restored."

Fin Man agreed, his resolve strengthening. He watched as the Coralyth the Radiant began to weave her magic, her hands moving in intricate patterns as she channeled the energy of the ocean.

The water around her began to glow, and a soft, soothing hum filled the air. Fin Man could feel the energy flowing into the coral, mending and growing the branches, while bringing color and life back to the reef.

The transformation was breathtaking. The bleached coral began to regain its vibrant hues, the brittle branches grew strong and sturdy, and the fish returned, filling the water with movement and color. The reef, once on the brink of death, was now coming back to life. To thrive once more.

But the Guardians' work was not yet done. She turned to Fin Man, her eyes filled with determination.

"The reef is healed, but it remains vulnerable," she said. "You must take this message to the surface world and tell them that the ocean is not a resource to be exploited, but a living, breathing entity that must be respected and protected. Only through unity can the coral, and all life within the sea, be saved."

With the Heart of the Sea glowing warmly in his hand, Fin Man knew that his next mission was clear. He would return to the surface and spread the message. He would set out and go forward, speaking to scientists, governments, and communities about the importance of the oceans.

He would fight for the protection of the reefs, advocating for policies that would reduce pollution, curb climate change, and promote sustainable fishing practices.

A New Beginning

As he swam back toward the shore, Fin Man felt a profound sense of fulfillment settle over him. The reef was safe—for now. But he understood that this victory was only the beginning. The greater battle to save the ocean had just begun.

The Elders and Coralyth had gifted him strength, wisdom, and purpose, yet the hardest task remained: inspiring humanity to listen, to change, and to act. That burden rested on his shoulders alone for now.

Fin Man needed more help. He knew that the journey ahead would be long, uncertain, and filled with trials. He felt no fear. He did, however, carry the blessing of the ocean's wisdom, the loyalty of the sea's creatures, and an unshakable belief that together, they could restore the fragile balance of life beneath the waves.

Fin Man was ready. And as the first rays of sunlight pierced the water, illuminating the now-thriving reef, Fin Man knew that he was on the right path.

The ocean had called him, and he had answered. Now, it was time to unite the world in the fight to protect the seas and ensure a future where coral could continue to flourish, bringing life and beauty to the depths for generations to come.

Chapter 4
The Tide of Resistance

After some success in restoring the coral reefs with the help of Coralyth, Fin Man's confidence grew, but so did the weight of the mission he had accepted.

The ocean was vast, and there were many troubles. The Elders and Coralyth made it clear that the real battle was not just in healing the ocean but in changing the hearts and minds of the people on land.

The next challenge would come not from the sea, but from those who profited from its exploitation.

And Fin Man had always known that he would need to confront the human world, but he hadn't anticipated just how difficult that task would be.

Returning to the shore, he took on the appearance of a normal man, his dolphin-like features receding, his skin no longer gray but a healthy tan.

He walked among the people, listening, learning, and preparing to share the message of the ocean's plight. But what he discovered disturbed him deeply.

The coastal cities were alive with industry. Massive fishing vessels crowded the harbors, their nets bulging with catches hauled from waters that once seemed endless.

Factories along the shoreline belched pollutants that bled into the sea, while towering rigs clawed oil from the ocean floor with relentless hunger. The air hung heavy with salt, smoke, and the faint metallic tang of machinery.

People rushed through their daily routines, blind to the silent catastrophe spreading beneath the waves—an unfolding tragedy hidden just beyond the shoreline's glitter.

Fin Man stood at the edge of the sprawling metropolis, a city whose prosperity depended on the very ocean it was slowly destroying.

Towering skyscrapers glittered in the sunlight, monuments of wealth forged from decades of extracting more from the ocean than it could sustain. This city was the throne room of power—home to corporations that ruled global fishing, oil extraction, and marine transport. Their influence stretched across continents and seas alike.

These industries not only fueled the city's economy, but they also posed some of the greatest threats to the ocean's survival.

It was here that Fin Man chose to make his stand. The Elders had gifted him the power of the ocean, but he knew this battle demanded more than ancient wisdom and magic—it required human cooperation.

If he could persuade the industry leaders who ruled this city to change their ways, the ripple effect could reshape the future of the seas.

Problems Beneath the Surface

During his investigations, Fin Man uncovered a crisis hidden from public view: thousands of unused and abandoned oil rigs scattered across the world's oceans. These rusting giants, left stagnant for years, leaked oil into the water, poisoning entire marine ecosystems. Each rig was a wound carved into the ocean's body, and the cost of ignoring them was catastrophic.

At a private meeting with industry leaders, Fin Man laid out his concerns.

"You've left these rigs to rot—pipelines rupturing, toxic remnants seeping into the sea. Do you understand what you're doing to the waters you claim to cherish?"

The CEOs exchanged skeptical glances. One of them, a woman in a sharply tailored suit, leaned forward.

"You talk as though we want to harm the ocean. These rigs are inactive; we've moved on to cleaner technologies.

What would you have us do? Spend millions to dismantle them when no one is watching?"

"You're not moving on," Fin Man countered, his voice sharp.

"You're leaving destruction in your wake, and the ocean suffers for it. Those rigs must be plugged or removed. Ignoring the problem isn't progress—it's negligence."

Fin Man presented solutions, drawing on advice from his father and human engineers committed to ocean restoration. He explained the process of well abandonment, also known as plugging and abandonment. (P&A)

"The rigs must be properly sealed to prevent oil leakage. Cement barriers can be placed deep within the wellbore to stop the flow of oil and gas. These structures should then be capped with a protective layer to withstand the ocean's pressure."

He went on to say, "Some rigs can be converted into artificial reefs, providing shelter for marine life. But this must only happen after they're thoroughly cleaned of toxic materials."

Fin Man described the careful process. Rigs would have to be dismantled one fragment at a time. Then their remnants would need to be reclaimed or laid to rest without harm.

"It demands great cost," he said, "but the ocean's future is worth nothing less."

One CEO, a gray-haired man with a gravelly voice, leaned back in his chair.

"These are noble ideas, but the reality is that such efforts are costly and complex. Who will fund this? The government? Us? You?"

Fin Man's eyes blazed with resolve. "You will fund the restoration efforts. Your industries have taken from the ocean's bounty for decades, and now you must answer for the damage left behind. This isn't charity—it's justice."

"Think of the goodwill this would generate. Consumers are becoming more conscious of sustainability. If your companies lead the way, others will follow, and you'll not only protect the ocean but also your reputations."

The CEOs were divided. Some saw the wisdom in Fin Man's words; others dismissed him as an idealist.

Fin Man used The Heart Of The Sea to display a holographic image of the ocean floor.

It showed the devastating effects of the leaking rigs—blackened waters, lifeless coral, and oil-slicked fish.

The room fell silent.

"This is what you're leaving behind?" Fin Man said, his deep voice reverberating.

"The ocean remembers. What legacy do you want to leave?"

Reluctantly, the CEOs agreed to a pilot program to address the abandoned rigs.

Fin Man offered to help, going forward to assist human engineers in sealing wells and cleaning debris.

The first rig to be decommissioned was a long-abandoned structure off the Gulf of Mexico.

Engineers labored tirelessly. Their work was guided and strengthened by The Elders' great knowledge and ancient abilities. The process was grueling. And it required days of cutting, sealing, and cleansing. But when the waters finally cleared, and the marine life began to return, the effort felt nothing short of miraculous.

As the news of the project spread, public support grew. Governments offered subsidies to encourage more companies to participate, and environmental organizations partnered with corporations to share the financial burden.

The pilot program expanded, and abandoned rigs across the globe were transformed from threats into opportunities for restoration.

Fin Man knew the fight was far from over, but the success of the initiative was a turning point. It showed that even the most entrenched industries could change when faced with the undeniable truth of their impact.

The Turning Point

Standing on the shoreline after the first rig was dismantled, Fin Man watched dolphins swim through the now-clear waters. "The ocean is resilient," he said softly. "But we must never forget that resilience isn't an excuse for recklessness. It's a call to do better."

Fin Man's arguments, backed by the wisdom of the Ocean Elders and the power of the Heart of the Sea, were compelling, but he quickly realized that he was up against more than just ignorance— he was facing greed, ambition, and a deep-seated resistance to change.

One of the most powerful men in the city was Maxwell Crane, CEO of Marinetek Industries. A company that controlled a vast portion of the world's fisheries and marine transportation.

Crane was known for his ruthlessness in business, his willingness to exploit every resource at his disposal to increase profits, and his disdain for those who stood in his way.

Fin Man knew that convincing Crane would be no small feat, but he also knew that if he could win him over, it would send a powerful message to the rest of the industry.

So, Fin Man arranged a meeting with Crane, using the influence he had gained from smaller victories along the way.

Crane had heard of Fin Man as his fame was growing, and he was intrigued by the young man who had begun to make waves in the environmental world, so he agreed.

The meeting took place in Crane's office, a towering skyscraper with sweeping views of the open sea. Below them stretched the very ocean his company depended on—an expanse both exploited and taken for granted.

Crane was a tall, imposing man with sharp features and piercing blue eyes that held no warmth. He sat behind a massive desk, flanked by screens displaying stock prices, market trends, and the latest reports from his global empire.

When Fin Man entered the room, Crane barely looked up; his attention was focused on the latest quarterly profits.

"So, you're the one causing all the noise," Crane said, finally looking up with a dismissive smile. "What can I do for you?"

Fin Man took a deep breath, feeling the weight of the Heart of the Sea pulsing in his pocket, reminding him of his purpose.

"Mr. Crane, I'm here to talk to you about the future—both yours and the oceans."

"The way things are going, we're on a path to destruction. The ocean is dying, and with it, everything we depend on. I'm asking you to change direction, to lead the way in protecting the seas rather than exploiting them."

Crane's smile faded, replaced by a look of cold indifference.

"The ocean is a resource, Mr. Fin Man, and like any resource, it's there to be used."

"My company employs thousands of people, feeds millions, and generates billions in revenue. I don't see why I should jeopardize all that for the sake of some fish."

"It's more than just fish," Fin Man replied, his voice firm.

"The ocean is the lifeblood of this planet. It regulates our climate, provides food, and supports a vast array of life. Without it, we're all doomed. The profits you're chasing now will mean nothing if the ocean collapses.

I'm not asking you to stop your business—I'm asking you to do it sustainably, to invest in the future rather than destroy it."

Crane leaned back in his chair, his eyes narrowing.

"Sustainability is a nice word, but it's expensive. And frankly, it's not my concern. My shareholders expect results, and that's what I deliver. If you want to save the ocean, go talk to someone else. I have a business to run."

Fin Man felt a surge of frustration, but he kept his composure.

"Mr. Crane, I've seen what's happening beneath the waves. I've spoken with Coralyth the Radiant, she is a Coral Guardian, and the Ocean Elders—beings far older and wiser than either of us.

They've shown me the future, and it's not one you want to be a part of. But it doesn't have to be that way. You have the power to change things. You can be a leader, not just in business, but in saving the world."

Crane's expression hardened.

"This meeting is over," he said, rising from his chair.

"I'm not interested in fairy tales about ocean spirits. The only future I'm concerned with is the one that keeps my company profitable.

And if you're smart, you'll stick to the environmental protests and leave the real work to people like me."

Fin Man stood, realizing that he had reached an impasse. But as he turned to leave, he couldn't resist one last attempt.

"Mr. Crane, the ocean is speaking to us. It's crying out for help. If we don't listen, we'll all pay the price.

Think about what I've said—before it's too late."

Crane didn't respond. His focus was already back on his screens as Fin Man left the office.

The door closed behind him with a finality that echoed in his mind. As he stepped out into the bustling streets, Fin Man felt a wave of despair. He had known this would be difficult, but he hadn't expected such resistance, such a refusal to even consider change.

But as he walked away from the skyscraper, the Heart of the Sea pulsed in his pocket, reminding him that the fight wasn't over. The ocean's call was still strong, and he knew he couldn't give up. There were others who would listen and understand the urgency of the situation.

And if he had to, he would find a way to bring the message directly to the people, bypassing those like Crane who refused to see beyond their own greed.

Fin Man knew that the path ahead would be filled with challenges, but he also knew that he was not alone. The Heart of the Sea in his pocket confirmed this.

The ocean was with him, and the Heart of the Sea was his guide. So, he looked out at the distant horizon, where the land met the water, feeling a renewed sense of determination.

The tide of resistance was strong, but Fin Man was stronger. He would continue his fight for the oceans and the creatures that called them home. He was fighting for the future of the world. And the journey was far from over. The battle to save the seas had only just begun.

Chapter 5
The Whispering Waters

After the disheartening encounter with Maxwell Crane, Fin Man knew that his approach needed to evolve.

The corporate world, driven by profit and detached from the natural world, was going to be a tough battleground. Yet, the ocean's cries were becoming louder in his heart, urging him to seek other avenues.

If he couldn't change the minds of the powerful, perhaps he could inspire the people and the everyday inhabitants of the world to take up the cause.

Determined to find a new way forward, Fin Man returned to the ocean, diving deep into its embrace where he felt most at peace.

The Heart of the Sea, nestled close to his chest, seemed to hum with anticipation, as if guiding him toward the next step in his journey. And as he swam, Fin Man felt the ocean itself responding to his presence. Currents gently nudging him in a specific direction, as if they too were alive and conscious.

He allowed the currents to guide him, knowing instinctively that they were leading him to something important.

Hours passed as he swam further from the shore, deeper into the wild, untouched parts of the ocean where few humans had ever ventured.

The water grew darker, the light from above dimming as he descended into a world of shadows and mystery. But Fin Man felt no fear; this was his realm, his home, and he knew that the ocean was leading him somewhere special.

After a while, he reached a vast, submerged forest of kelp, its tall, swaying fronds creating a maze-like labyrinth that seemed to stretch on forever.

And as Fin Man navigated through the dense foliage, he heard a sound, faint at first but growing clearer as he approached—a soft, melodic whisper that seemed to echo through the water.

Soon, the whispers grew louder and more distinct. Fin Man realized they weren't just random sounds; they were words and voices speaking in a language as old as the ocean itself.

They called to him, beckoning him deeper into the kelp forest, urging him to listen.

At the heart of the forest, Fin Man found a clearing where the kelp parted to reveal a large, circular pool of crystal-clear water.

The whispers were growing louder now, resonating from the water itself. And Fin Man knew he had found the source. He swam to the center of the pool and listened, closing his eyes as the voices washed over him like a gentle tide.

"We are the Whispering Waters," the voices said in unison, their tone soft yet filled with ancient wisdom.

"We are the memories of the ocean, the keepers of its secrets, and the voice of its soul. We have watched over these waters for millennia, and we have seen the rise and fall of countless beings.

We have called you here, Fin Man, because the ocean needs you now more than ever."

Fin Man opened his eyes, looking into the depths of the pool. He could see faint images forming in the water—scenes from the past, present, and possible futures, all intertwined in a complex tapestry of light and shadow.

He saw the birth of the ocean, the emergence of life, and the evolution of countless species.

He also saw the damage done by humanity. The pollution, the overfishing, the destruction of habitats, and more.

And then, he saw something new—images of hope. Where people were coming together to heal the ocean. He was seeing a world where the balance was restored.

"What must I do?" Fin Man asked, his voice filled with both awe and determination.

The Whispering Waters responded; their voices gentle but insistent.

"You must be our messenger, Fin Man.

The ocean's voice is drowned out by the noise of the human world, but you can make it heard.

You must show the people the truth. Not just with words, but with actions that resonate with their hearts.

The time has come to awaken the Guardians of the Shore."

"Guardians of the Shore?" Fin Man repeated, his voice sounding intrigued.

"Yes," the Whispering Waters replied.

"They are the spirits of the coastal lands, protectors of the boundary between sea and land. They have the power to influence the hearts of those who live by the water, to remind them of their connection to the ocean.

But they have been dormant for many years, forgotten by most. You must find them, awaken them, and bring them to the surface world."

Fin Man felt a surge of hope. The Whispering Waters were giving him a way forward, along with a new plan to unite the people of the land with the ocean's cause.

But he also knew that finding the Guardians would not be easy.

They were scattered along the coasts of the world, hidden in places where the natural world still held sway.

"Where do I begin?" Fin Man asked, ready to take on this new challenge.

"Start where the ocean meets the land," the Whispering Waters instructed.

"Seek out the places where the bond between sea and shore runs deepest—ancient coves, sacred beaches, cliffs that have stood watch for millennia.

The Guardians are there, sleeping and waiting for someone with the heart and soul of the ocean to call them forth.

But beware, Fin Man, for there are forces that will try to stop you. Forces that thrive on the chaos and destruction of the ocean. They will not want the Guardians awakened."

Fin Man nodded, feeling the weight of the mission settle on his shoulders, but also the determination to see it through.

He thanked the Whispering Waters for their guidance, and with a final glance into the depths of the pool, he turned and swam back through the kelp forest, his mind racing with possibilities.

The journey ahead would take him to the farthest reaches of the world, to places where the land and sea intertwined in ways that were as ancient as time itself.

His mission was clear: to awaken the Guardians and unite them with the people of the shore. Only together could they stand against the forces gathering to threaten the ocean's future.

As Fin Man emerged from the water, the setting sun cast a golden glow over the waves. He felt a renewed sense of purpose.

The ocean had spoken to him once more, and he had answered its call.

The Whispering Waters had shown him the way forward, and now it was up to him to see it through.

The battle to save the seas was far from over, but Fin Man knew that with the help of the Guardians of the Shore and the people of the world, victory was within reach.

The tide was again turning, and Fin Man was ready to lead the charge.

Chapter 6
The Guardians Awaken

With the guidance of the Whispering Waters echoing in his mind, Fin Man set out on a new quest: to awaken the Guardians of the Shore.

These ancient spirits were protectors of the boundary between land and sea, and were key to uniting humanity with the ocean's cause. They had the power to remind people of their deep, intrinsic connection to the water and to inspire a collective effort to heal the seas.

A New Journey Begins

Fin Man's journey began along the rugged coastlines of Central America, this is a place where the land and sea had danced together for centuries.

The first location he sought was a sacred beach known to the locals as "La Playa del Alma"— The Beach of the Soul.

It was said to be a place where the ocean's spirit was particularly strong, where the waves whispered secrets to those who listened closely enough.

As he arrived at the beach, Fin Man could immediately sense the ancient energy that permeated the area.

The shoreline was lined with smooth, polished stones, each one etched with symbols that spoke of the ocean's timeless wisdom.

The air was thick with the scent of salt and the rhythmic sound of waves crashing against the shore. The beach was deserted, as if it had been waiting just for him.

Fin Man walked along the water's edge, feeling the pull of the Heart of the Sea growing stronger with every step.

The ocean seemed to pulse in time with his heartbeat, guiding him toward a particular spot where the sand met the sea.

Here, the water was unusually clear, and the waves lapped gently against the ocean shore as if in greeting him personally.

He knelt by the water, placing his hand on the wet sand, and closed his eyes. The Whispering Waters had told him that the Guardians could be awakened by those who carried the ocean's soul within them, and Fin Man knew that this was his moment to call them forth.

He spoke softly, his voice blending with the sound of the waves.

"Guardians of the Shore, hear me. The oceans need you now, more than ever.

Rise from your slumber and join me in the fight to protect the seas.

"The time has come to remind humanity of its ancient bond with the waters—to heal the rift between land and sea. I call upon you now... awaken."

For a moment, nothing happened. The beach remained still, the waves gentle and unchanging.

But then, Fin Man felt a shift in the air, a subtle change in the energy around him. The water at his feet began to glow with a soft, ethereal light, and the symbols on the stones lining the shore started to shimmer.

Slowly, the water in front of him began to swirl, forming a small whirlpool that grew in size and intensity.

Then from the center of the whirlpool, a figure began to emerge—a being of pure water, shaped like a human but with flowing tendrils of seaweed for hair and eyes that glowed with the light of the ocean depths.

The figure rose from the sea, standing before Fin Man with an aura of ancient power.

"I am Callista, Guardian of the Shore," the figure spoke, her voice like the rush of the tide.

"You have awakened me, Fin Man, and I sense the urgency in your heart. The ocean is in peril, and the balance must be restored. I will stand with you, and together we will remind the people of their duty to the sea."

Fin Man felt a wave of relief wash over him. He had succeeded in awakening another Guardian, but he knew there were more to be found.

Callista's presence was a powerful ally, but the ocean needed the strength of all the Guardians united.

"Thank you, Callista," Fin Man replied, his voice filled with gratitude."

Then spoke Callista again, "I have been told by The Elders that you have already awakened and met with Coralyth the Radiant. Now we must awaken the other Guardians, scattered along the coasts of the world."

Fin Man replied, "Will you help me find them?" Callista nodded, her eyes glowing with determination.

"Yes, Fin Man. I will help you. I know where my fellow Guardians rest. And we need the power of all of the Guardians, including Coralyth.

We must travel to the cliffs of Ireland, the coves of Australia, the fjords of Norway, and the sands of Egypt. Each of these places holds a Guardian, and together, we will awaken them all."

Fin Man replied, "Yes, Coralyth will meet us along the way."

Now with Callista by his side, Fin Man felt a renewed sense of purpose. The journey ahead would be long and challenging, but with each Guardian they awaken, their strength will grow.

Their first destination was the cliffs of Ireland, where the Guardian known as Bradan slept. As they journeyed, Fin Man reflected on the importance of uniting all the Guardians.

Only together could they influence the hearts and minds of those on land and inspire a movement powerful enough to turn the tide in favor of the ocean.

So Fin Man, Coralyth, and Callista set out at once, traveling swiftly across vast waters, carried by the ocean currents that rose and curled in response to Callista's command.

Days blurred into nights as he traveled beneath moonlit swells and storm-tossed skies, guided by the faint pulse of ancient magic that called him ever northward. Migrating whales sang warnings of distant dangers, while schools of silver fish parted before him like living pathways. Even the tides seemed to shift in his favor, urging him onward.

Ahead lay the rugged Irish coast with its jagged cliffs rising like the ribs of the earth itself. Somewhere within those stone walls, Bradan waited, dreaming in the deep. And Fin Man knew that awakening this Guardian would be the next step in restoring balance to the world.

The cliffs were said to be a place of great power, where the land met the sea in a dramatic, towering embrace. It was a place where the waves crashed against the rocks with such force that the sound could be heard for miles.

As they approached the Irish coast, the air grew colder, and the waves became rougher, as if the sea itself was challenging them.

Soon, the cliffs rose before them, dark and imposing, with the waves crashing violently against their base.

Fin Man could feel the presence of the Guardian deep within the cliffs, a powerful force that had been dormant for centuries.

"This is where Bradan sleeps," Callista said, her voice cutting through the roar of the waves.

"He is the Guardian of strength and resilience. He has the power to withstand any storm, and his presence will be crucial in our battle to protect the seas."

Fin Man nodded, steeling himself for the task ahead.

Together, they approached the base of the cliffs, where a narrow, jagged path led up to a small, hidden cave. Thick, tangled vines and moss almost completely concealed the entrance to the cave, but Fin Man could feel the energy emanating from within.

With Callista and Coralyth beside him, Fin Man ascended the ancient path, the wind swirling like a living force as if urging them onward.

When they reached the cave, Fin Man placed his hand on the cool, damp stone at its entrance, feeling the ancient power that lay within.

"Bradan, Guardian of the Cliffs, I call upon you to awaken," Fin Man said, his voice firm and resolute.

"The ocean needs your strength. And the time has come to rise and join the fight to protect the seas."

For a moment, there was only silence. Then, the ground beneath them began to tremble, and the sound of cracking stone echoed through the cave.

The vines at the entrance began to move, parting to reveal a deep, glowing light within.

And from the cave, a massive figure emerged, towering over Fin Man, Coralyth, and Callista.

Bradan was a being of rock and water, his body made of the very cliffs he had protected for centuries. His eyes were like glowing embers, filled with the fire of the earth itself.

"I have heard your call, Fin Man," Bradan rumbled, his voice like the grinding of stone.

"The ocean's plight has reached even my deep slumber. I will lend you my strength, for the sea and the land are one. Together, we will stand against those who seek to harm the ocean."

Fin Man felt a surge of hope as Bradan joined them. With Callista's wisdom, Coralyth's powers, and Bradan's strength, their group was growing more formidable. But there were still more Guardians to find, and the clock was ticking.

The forces that threatened the ocean were growing stronger, and the task of uniting the world in its defense was daunting.

Their next destination was the sun-drenched coves of Australia, where the Guardian Marra slept beneath ancient tides.

The coastline shimmered with heat and color—opal waters, red stone cliffs, and beaches that seemed to glow with their own inner fire.

Leaving the Irish cliffs behind, Fin Man, Coralyth, Braden, and Callista slipped once more into the open sea.

Bradan's awakening had stirred the waters, and the ocean seemed to pulse with renewed strength as they traveled south. The cold northern currents carried them past towering sea stacks and through swirling mists, where ancient seabirds cried overhead like guardians of forgotten lore.

As they moved farther from Ireland, the waters warmed. They crossed vast stretches of open ocean where the horizon curved like the edge of the world. Some nights, the sky blazed with stars so bright they reflected on the waves like scattered pearls. Other nights, storms rose without warning—walls of wind and rain that tested their resolve. Yet the sea always parted for them in the end, guided by Callista's command and Bradan's steady presence echoing behind them.

They passed migrating whales whose deep songs vibrated through Fin Man's bones, carrying messages of distant coasts and shifting tides. Schools of glowing plankton lit their path in shimmering blues and greens, turning the water into a living constellation. Even the currents themselves seemed to whisper encouragement, urging them onward toward the next Guardian.

And as they moved toward Australia, Fin Man couldn't help but think about the enormity of the task before them.

He understood that calling the Guardians forth was merely the first step. The greater task would be awakening humanity itself, reminding them that the ocean was not a treasure to plunder, but the very force that sustained their world.

He had many questions on how this would be achieved, but with each Guardian they awakened, Fin Man felt the possibilities were endless. Together, it could be done.

The ocean's voice was growing louder now, its power stronger, and with some of the Guardians by his side, he knew they had a chance—a chance to save the seas, and in doing so, save the world.

Chapter 7
The Life Giver

The journey to the sun-drenched coves of Australia was both exhilarating and daunting.

The energy of the ocean around Fin Man and his growing team of Guardians was palpable, a mixture of urgency and hope.

Marra was the Guardian of life, a spirit deeply connected to the vibrant ecosystems of the ocean, from the smallest plankton to the largest whales. Her power was crucial in restoring the balance of life in the seas.

Fin Man knew that with Marra's help, they could begin to heal the wounds inflicted on the marine world.

As they approached the Australian coast, the water around them shifted from deep blue to a lighter, more vibrant hue, teeming with life.

Schools of fish darted through coral reefs, and the sunlit shallows sparkled like a treasure trove of aquatic wonders.

Yet, beneath this beauty, Fin Man could sense the fragility of the ecosystem. The reef was not as vibrant as it once was, and there were signs of bleaching, a stark reminder of the challenges they faced.

Callista and Bradan, who had become Fin Man's trusted allies, swam alongside him, their presence a source of strength. Coralyth followed from behind. And Bradan's massive, rock-like form moved with surprising grace through the water from a distance.

"This is where Marra rests," Callista said, her voice filled with reverence. Her fluid, water-like body seemed to merge seamlessly with the ocean around her.

"She is the life force of the ocean, the pulse that sustains all living creatures within it. And without her, the ocean's ability to regenerate and thrive is greatly diminished."

Fin Man nodded; he knew how much was at stake.

The cove they approached was a secluded area, hidden from the world by towering cliffs and dense mangroves.

The water was so clear that it reflected the sky like a mirror, but as Fin Man gazed into its depths, he could see the outlines of the coral below—faded, brittle, and dying.

"This place was once a sanctuary," Bradan rumbled, his voice filled with sorrow.

"But even sanctuaries can be harmed when the balance is lost."

Fin Man felt the weight of the Heart of the Sea against his chest, its pulse quickening as they neared the heart of the cove.

He knew what he had to do. So he swam to the center of the cove and hovered above the coral reef with Coralyth, his eyes closed, as he reached out with his senses, feeling the life that remained.

"Marra," he called softly, his voice carrying through the water.

"Guardian of Life, I call upon you to awaken. The ocean needs your power to heal, to bring life back to these waters. Please, hear my call."

For a moment, nothing happened. The cove remained still, while the water was gently lapping against the shore.

But then, Fin Man felt a change in the current, a subtle shift that grew stronger with each passing second. The water around him began to glow with a soft, green light, and the coral beneath him started to shimmer, as if waking from a deep slumber.

From the depths of the reef, a figure began to emerge.

Marra's form was both beautiful and awe-inspiring, her body composed of living coral and flowing seaweed, with skin that shimmered like the scales of a fish. Her hair was a cascade of bioluminescent tendrils, glowing with the light of the ocean's deepest secrets.

Her eyes, like twin pearls, radiated a warmth and wisdom that spoke of the countless lives she had nurtured.

"Fin Man," Marra's voice was gentle yet powerful, like the caress of a wave on a warm summer day.

"I have felt the ocean's pain, the suffering of the creatures within it. It has weighed heavily on my heart, but your call has reached me.

You seek to restore the balance, to heal the wounds of the ocean. I will join you in this quest."

Fin Man felt a surge of hope as Marra's presence filled the cove. The water around them seemed to come alive. Now it was vibrant and full of energy, as if responding to Marra's very essence.

Fin Man noticed with Marra's and Coralyth's presence that the coral began to regain its color, the fish swam with renewed vigor, and the once-fading life of the cove started to bloom again.

"We must act quickly," Marra continued, her voice tinged with urgency.

The ocean is a single living system, and a wound in one region weakens the whole. Our task is to restore balance everywhere, not only on this shore."

It will take time, and it will take the cooperation of all living beings—both in the sea and on the land."

Fin Man nodded, his resolve stronger than ever. "We'll start here, with this cove. We'll make it a symbol of what can be achieved when we work together to heal the ocean. And then we'll spread that message to the world."

Bradan stepped forward, his massive form casting a shadow over the reef.

"I will lend my strength to protect this place, to ensure that the balance we restore here is not disrupted again."

"And I will continue to guide you," Callista added, her voice calm and steady.

"Together, we will awaken the remaining Guardians and unite the world in this cause."

Marra smiled, her eyes shining with hope.

"Thank you, my friends. With our combined power, we can begin the process of renewal. But we must also be vigilant, for there are forces that will seek to undo our work. The darkness that threatens the ocean will not rest, and neither can we."

With Marra's words in mind, Fin Man began to work alongside the other Guardians to restore the cove.

Coralyth extended her hands over the reef, and warm, golden light flowed from her being like liquid sunlight. The coral responded instantly—bleached branches flushing with color, fractured structures knitting themselves whole. Kelp forests unfurled in slow, graceful spirals, rising toward the surface as if waking from a long sleep. Fish darted through the rejuvenated growth, their scales shimmering with renewed life.

Bradan reinforced the natural defenses of the cove, channeling his immense strength into the stone itself. The cliffs groaned and shifted under his touch, cracks sealing and weak points knitting together as if the earth were healing from within. Boulders settled into new, protective formations, creating barriers that softened the force of incoming waves and shielded the fragile ecosystem tucked safely behind them.

Marra lifted her hands, and a warm, golden glow rippled outward. Schools of fish gathered as if drawn by an ancient memory.

And Callista whispered to the currents, and they obeyed. From far below, ancient streams surged upward, swirling around her in powerful spirals. They carried the ocean's hidden nourishment. Minerals and nutrients, warmth, and life itself. All pouring over the reef like a blessing.

In the days that followed, the cove changed before their eyes. The reef, once pale and failing, flourished into a radiant haven, teeming with creatures drawn to its restored vitality.

Word soon carried across the coastal communities, and people journeyed from every corner of the region to see the reborn cove. The sight stirred something within them—wonder at the ocean's beauty, and a renewed belief in the resilience of the world they had nearly forgotten.

Fin Man understood that this was just the beginning. The cove was a symbol of hope and a testament to what could be achieved when people and nature worked together.

But their work was far from finished. The remaining Guardians still slept, and the call to protect the ocean had to reach every corner of the world.

As the sun set over the newly restored cove, casting a golden glow over the water, Fin Man stood with the Guardians by his side, looking out at the horizon.

The journey ahead was unknown, and the challenges were great, but he knew that they were on the right path.

The ocean was beginning to heal, and with the Guardians' guidance, its renewed strength would endure for generations to come.

It was clear now that the tides were turning, and Fin Man stood ready to lead the charge in the battle to save the seas.

With Marra's life-giving power, Bradan's unshakable strength, Coralyth's radiant energy, and Callista's ancient wisdom, Fin Man felt a surge of purpose rising within him—a force unlike anything the ocean had witnessed in ages. Together, they would awaken the remaining Guardians and stand against the powers determined to tear the sea apart.

The future of the oceans and the world beyond them depended on what they chose to do next.

Chapter 8
The Voice of the Depths

With the restoration of the cove in Australia, Fin Man and his team of Guardians had achieved their first major victory. The vibrant life teeming within the once-fading reef was a beacon of hope, a testament to the power of unity and determination. Yet as Fin Man gazed out at the horizon, he contemplated what was next. The ocean's survival required more than isolated successes—it demanded a global awakening.

Plastic pollution in the ocean was devastating in scale, its impact stretching far beyond the Great Pacific Garbage Patch. This infamous "plastic dump," located in the North Pacific Ocean between California and Hawaii, was a glaring reminder of humanity's negligence, with ocean currents concentrating vast amounts of debris into a swirling, toxic gyre. Yet Fin Man understood that plastic pollution wasn't confined to a single area; it plagued every ocean gyre and every coastline, threatening ecosystems and marine life worldwide.

Their next destination was the fjords of Norway, where the Guardian known as Aegir slumbered. Aegir, the Guardian of the Depths, was a being of profound wisdom and mystery, holding knowledge of the ocean's ancient ways. His connection to the seas made him an invaluable ally in the fight to protect the marine world from further destruction.

The journey to Norway was long, taking Fin Man and the Guardians through the vast waters of the Pacific and Atlantic Oceans.

Along the way, the scars of humanity's impact were undeniable—plastic debris littered the surface, oil slicks tainted the water, and lifeless zones, once thriving with biodiversity, served as haunting reminders of the ocean's fragility.

Each sight strengthened Fin Man's resolve to press on. As they traveled, the team exchanged ideas, shaping a vision for real change. Callista spoke of community-driven cleanups and global coalitions, while Bradan argued for advanced technologies capable of intercepting plastics before they ever reached the sea.

As the group was nearing the Norwegian coast, the temperature dropped, and winter's gloom settled over the sky. The fjords rose like colossal sentinels, their cliffs plunging into waters as dark as midnight. This was a place carved by time itself—ancient, secretive, and alive with mysteries waiting beneath the waves.

"This place feels timeless," Fin Man remarked as they entered the fjord. The stillness of the water was almost reverent, as if aware of the power lying beneath.

"Aegir has slumbered here for centuries," Callista said in a hushed tone. "He is the keeper of the ocean's deepest secrets and the guardian of the abyss. Awakening him requires great need and reverence."

Fin Man nodded, understanding the gravity of their task. They were not merely calling upon a Guardian but awakening a force that had shaped the ocean's very fabric.

As they ventured deeper into the fjord, the water seemed to grow heavier, the weight of the depths pressing against them.

Bradan led the way, his imposing form cutting confidently through the cold water. Marra followed, her light casting warmth and life in the gloom. Coralyth followed from behind, pulsating energy forward. And Callista remained close to Fin Man, her sharp eyes scanning for any sign of Aegir's presence.

At the heart of the fjord, where cliffs nearly blocked out the sky, the water was a mirror of blackness, reflecting the towering rocks above. Fin Man felt the presence of Aegir deep below—a vast, ancient consciousness stirring faintly at their arrival.

"This is it," Fin Man whispered, placing a hand over the Heart of the Sea, which pulsed gently against his chest, resonating with the power of the depths. He closed his eyes and reached out with his mind, channeling all his love for the ocean, his hope for its future, and his determination to protect it.

"Aegir, Guardian of the Depths, hear me," Fin Man's voice echoed through the water. "The ocean is in peril. Plastic pollution chokes its surface, oil poisons its lifeblood, and humanity forgets its connection to the sea. We need your wisdom and your strength to restore balance and protect what remains. I call upon you to awaken."

For a long moment, silence hung heavy in the fjord. Then, the water began to churn, rippling as a deep, resonant sound rose from the depths. It was a sound like no other—a low, powerful hum that vibrated through the water and into their bones.

From the blackness below, a colossal shadow emerged, rising steadily. The water shimmered with an ethereal light as Aegir appeared, his form an imposing amalgam of swirling water and ancient, barnacle-encrusted stone. His eyes glowed like deep-sea vents, holding the fiery intensity of the earth's core.

"Aegir has awoken," Callista whispered in awe.

The Guardian of the Depths towered above them, his presence both humbling and magnificent. He gazed at Fin Man with eyes that seemed to pierce through time itself.

"Fin Man," Aegir's voice was a deep rumble, like the shifting of tectonic plates.

"You have disturbed my rest. I have heard the ocean's cry. The world above forgets the depths, discards its refuse into the sea, and allows the balance to crumble. Why should I rise for humanity's recklessness?"

Fin Man met Aegir's gaze, unflinching. "Because the ocean is more than a dumping ground.

It is the lifeblood of this planet, and we fight to remind humanity of that truth. With your power and wisdom, we can begin to heal these wounds and restore the ocean's vitality."

Aegir was silent, his massive form shifting subtly as if considering the plea. The swirling water around him carried the weight of his deliberation. Finally, he spoke, his voice resonating with resolve.

"I will join you," Aegir said, his tone a blend of warning and promise. "But the ocean's power is untamed, its balance fragile. Tread carefully, for the depths are as unpredictable as they are vast."

Fin Man bowed his head in respect. "Together, we will ensure the ocean's voice is heard, and its balance is restored."

With Aegir's agreement, Fin Man felt a renewed sense of purpose. The Guardian of the Depths had joined their cause, bringing the ancient wisdom and unparalleled power of the deep ocean. Their mission was growing, and with Aegir's support, they had taken a monumental step forward in the fight to protect the seas.

As the fjord fell silent once more, Fin Man couldn't help but feel both awe and responsibility for the power they had awakened. The ocean's future was uncertain, but with the Guardians united, hope was alive.

Aegir's presence was a reminder of the ocean's vastness, its ability to endure and survive even in the face of immense challenges.

But it was also a reminder of the responsibility they bore—to protect that power, and to ensure that it was used for good.

The Secrets That Rest

Their next destination was Egypt, where the final Guardian awaited.

The sands of the Egyptian coast held secrets of their own, ancient knowledge that had been passed down through the ages.

The Guardian who rested there, known as Anuket, was the Guardian of the Tides, a spirit deeply connected to the flow of rivers and currents and to the life-giving power of freshwater.

As they traveled towards Egypt, Fin Man reflected on the journey so far. Each Guardian they had awakened brought them closer to their goal, but each also presented new challenges and responsibilities.

The ocean was a vast, interconnected web of life, and the work of restoring its balance was only just beginning.

Aegir, now an integral part of their team, shared insights that expanded their understanding of the depths below the ocean's surface and it's many needs.

His wisdom was a reminder that the Guardians could not succeed alone. All efforts required the essential help of humanity.

"We must engage those who dwell on land," Aegir said during the journey. "The currents cannot cleanse themselves, nor can the rivers cease their flow of pollution without intervention. Humanity must learn to see itself as part of the ocean's story—not its master."

Fin Man agreed.

Their efforts were evolving, yet real transformation would require more than the Guardians' strength—it demanded the creativity and determination of humanity itself.

On their way to the shores of Egypt, Fin Man convinced the Guardians to chart their next move.

They would address what is known as the Great Pacific Garbage Patch. This dire symbol of ocean pollution was only one part of the larger crisis.

The plastic flowing into the oceans through rivers had to be intercepted at its source, preventing the relentless cycle of pollution.

"I am aware of a human initiative called 'The Ocean Cleanup,'" Marra said, her voice bright with hope.

"They've developed technologies to capture plastic in the gyres and to stop new pollution by installing barriers in rivers. Perhaps we can amplify their efforts."

Aegir, his deep voice resonating like the currents he commanded, added,

"The Guardians together with Fin Man can aid this cause."

Aegir went on to say, "Anuket's domain includes the rivers that carry this waste. She can enhance these barriers with natural forces—currents, tides, and winds—to make them more effective."

Fin Man nodded. "It's not just about cleaning up what's already there—it's about stopping more plastic from entering the oceans in the first place. If we combine human ingenuity with the Guardians' powers, we can tackle this problem from all sides."

The Flow Unbroken

When they arrived in Egypt, the sun cast an orange reddish glow over the coastline.

The Nile Delta stretched before them, its waters carrying the hopes and burdens of a nation. This was a sacred place—where river met sea, and where life had flowed unbroken for thousands of years.

It was here that Anuket of the Tides slept. Her presence tied to the lifeblood of the rivers. Especially bound to the flourishing of the Nile, she rested at the edge of the Nile Delta, where freshwater braided itself into the salt-rich breath of the Mediterranean.

She was the keeper of balance, the one who guided the mingling of waters so life could flourish in the in-between.

Fin Man spoke out, saying, "Anuket of the Tides, awaken and bless us with your presence."

For a moment, there was only the sound of the Nile moving steadily toward the sea as if listening. And then a figure emerged—luminous and fluid, her form ever-shifting like the currents she commanded.

The waters began to tremble. Silt lifted in slow spirals, reeds bowed as if recognizing an old power, and a soft shimmer spread across the surface like moonlight breaking through.

Anuket rose from the water, her body composed of flowing light and clear river water. Her presence both gentle and immense.

"I have heard your call," she said, her voice like a living stream—soothing, yet resolute.

Fin Man spoke firmly, "The waters are out of balance, and the life they sustain is in danger. Will you help us?"

Anuket replied, "You seek my aid to heal the ocean, but know this—restoring balance is not merely a task for the Guardians. It requires harmony between land and sea, and the cooperation of all who call this planet their home."

Fin Man stepped forward, his resolve unwavering. "We understand, Anuket. That's why we're here—to unite your power with the efforts of humanity."

From the heart of the estuary, Anuket of the Tides form carried the strength of the river and the rhythm of the sea, woven together in perfect balance. When she opened her eyes, the tides shifted in response, and the estuary exhaled.

Anuket of the Tides moved with the quiet authority of a threshold where worlds meet. Her presence shimmered like brackish water at dusk—part river, part sea, wholly alive with shifting currents. And around her, the water carried the pulse of both realms: the freshwater's steady push, and the ocean's rhythmic pull.

When she lifted her being, the tides responded, weaving together nutrients, silt, and light into a swirling veil of renewal, breathing in harmony as she tended the delicate dance of change, transition, and rebirth.

In her domain, every tide was a promise, and every meeting of waters carried the memory of beginnings. Now the river pulsed with quiet power, its currents heavy with history, memory, and need.

"We need you." Fin Man said, his voice steady. "The rivers and oceans are in danger. Pollution, climate change, and misuse threaten the sources of life itself. We must restore balance and protect the waters that sustain us all."

He went on to say, "Anuket of the Tides, you are the true Guardian of the Nile, protector of life. We seek your wisdom! Please join us in restoring balance to the world's waters."

Anuket listened, her form shimmering.

Then Fin Man explained, "There's a project already working to intercept plastic in rivers before it reaches the ocean. With your guidance, we can magnify its impact. This is a technology of river interceptors and floating barriers designed to trap plastic debris.

Her form shimmered again, as she listened with understanding.

"Humans have shown ingenuity," she said thoughtfully. "But their tools alone cannot solve this crisis. With my power, I can strengthen these barriers, ensuring that no waste escapes. And with the rivers themselves, I can guide the currents to carry the debris toward these interceptors rather than destruction."

"Together, we can turn rivers into allies," Marra imparted. Her voice was bright with hope.

Anuket nodded, while the golden light within her intensified.

Marra expressed, "We can create a network of protection, where the waters are no longer conduits of destruction but pathways of renewal." Her voice was filled with optimism.

Anuket nodded, while the shimmering light of her form flowed vividly.

"Very well. I will lend my strength to this cause. But humans must do their part. They must understand that the rivers and oceans are not endless repositories for waste but living entities in need of care and respect."

Anuket nodded again, the golden light within her growing brighter.

And so it began.

First, Anuket used her power to guide the currents of the Nile, strengthening the river flow to carry debris into the interceptors.

Aegir worked with the ocean currents, aligning floating barriers to maximize the collection into the gyres.

Callista reached out to the riverside communities, moving among them not as a distant Guardian but as a guide and listener.

She gathered elders, fishermen, families, and children along the banks, helping them see the river not as a resource to be used up, but as a living partner in their survival.

She taught simple, practical changes to the people, emphasizing how reducing single-use plastics at markets and homes could protect the waters that fed their crops and fisheries, as well as how waste could be collected and redirected before it ever reached the river. She described how small acts, repeated daily, could ripple outward into lasting change.

Callista centered herself to work with local leaders and teachers too, helping establish river clean-up days, education programs, and shared agreements to protect the banks from dumping and erosion. She encouraged the use of reusable materials and supported community recycling efforts. She helped create safe disposal points upstream, where pollution often began unnoticed.

But more than rules or systems, she restored reverence.

Through stories and quiet moments by the water's edge, she reminded people of the Nile's ancient role as giver of life. And the children learned to listen to the river's rhythms.

Fishermen learned to read its health. Families began to understand that protecting the river meant protecting themselves.

Slowly, attitudes shifted. And what had once been ignored became guarded. What had been taken for granted became treasured.

As the communities changed, so did the river—responding to care with clarity, to respect renewal by proving that true restoration always begins at the source.

Anuket, and the other Guardians and Fin Man were amazed and thrilled by all of this, imagining all that they may do going forward.

And certainly, now with Anuket's agreement, the Guardians and Fin Man could begin coordinating more of their efforts toward the entire ocean cleanup.

Many needs would continue to be met day by day. Slowly and steadily, the waters could heal.

The waters were healing.

The results were immediate and profound. Rivers that once carried tons of plastic waste began to run clearer.

And the floating barriers in the ocean, now bolstered by the Guardians' influence, captured debris at an unprecedented rate. But even as progress was made, Fin Man and the Guardians knew their work was far from over.

Restoring balance required not only technology with mystic intervention, but also a continual shift in humanity's mindset—a deeper understanding of its connection to the natural world. Humanity was the biggest challenge.

Prepared for what was next, Fin Man stood on the Egyptian coastline, watching the sunset over the sea.

The tide was turning—not only for the oceans, but for the planet itself.

Together with humanity, the Guardians had begun something extraordinary: a single awakening, a shared responsibility, and a future where the waters of the world could once again flow with life.

Chapter 9
The Keeper of the Waters

The desert sands of Egypt stretched out before Fin Man and the Guardians, a vast golden expanse shaped by wind, time, and endurance.

The air was dry and hot—a stark contrast to the cool, life-giving waters they had just helped restore. Yet beneath the arid surface of this ancient land flowed the power that had sustained civilizations for millennia.

Behind them, the Nile and the Delta glimmered—renewed, vibrant, alive.

Anuket stood with them now, no longer hidden within the river but fully present, her luminous form flowing softly like moving water beneath sunlight. Her power hummed through the land, steady and watchful, woven once more into the balance between river and sea.

Fin Man felt the Heart of the Sea pulse calmly against his chest. The connection between ocean and river was no longer theoretical—it was living, visible, undeniable. The Nile was flowing as it was meant to flow, carrying nourishment instead of waste, promise instead of harm.

"The Nile has always been a lifeline," Callista said quietly, gazing across the fertile banks where water met land. "What we see now is what happens when balance is honored."

Bradan nodded. "But balance must be protected. The threats remain—pollution upstream, overuse, and short-sighted decisions. Restoration is not a moment. It's a commitment."

Anuket turned toward them, her voice gentle but firm.

"The waters will respond as long as they are respected. Rivers remember how they were treated. So do oceans."

Marra stepped closer, her presence warm with resolve.

"What we've done here proves what's possible. The rivers can become allies again—not pathways of destruction, but channels of renewal."

Together, they reviewed the work already set in motion.

The river interceptors now stood fortified under Anuket's guidance, their purpose sharpened as currents subtly shifted to carry waste toward collection instead of the open sea.

Along the Mediterranean coast, ocean barriers, shaped by Aegir's steady influence, moved in quiet harmony with the natural tides, working with the water rather than against it.

Communities along the Nile had begun to respond as well. Inspired by the river's renewal, people took ownership of their waterways, reducing plastic use and protecting what sustained them.

The results were undeniable.

Waters once clouded ran clear. Fish returned. Birds nested along the banks. The land itself seemed to breathe again.

Word spread quickly—of a river healed, and of hope restored.

But Fin Man knew this victory was only one chapter in a far greater story.

"The Nile is flowing again," he said, watching the sun lower over the delta. "But the world's waters are still in danger. What we've done here must happen everywhere."

Anuket met his gaze. "And it will—if you continue," she said. "Balance is fragile, but it is also resilient when protected."

As dusk settled in, the Guardians stood together at the river's edge. They had awakened the final Guardian. Their circle was now complete. And together they made a vow, beneath the darkening sky:

That they would not rest until the balance of the world's waters was restored.

They would stand against those who treated rivers and oceans as expendable.

They would ensure that the future generations would inherit a world where water—fresh and salt—continued to sustain life.

Alas, as they turned toward their next destination, Fin Man felt it clearly now—the voice of the waters growing stronger, the planet itself beginning to listen.

The tide was turning.

And together—Fin Man, Anuket, and the other Guardians were ready to lead the way.

Chapter 10
The Awakening

With the awakening of Anuket, the final Guardian, Fin Man and his team had completed a monumental task.

The Guardians were united, each contributing their unique powers to the mission of restoring balance to the world's waters.

The transformation of the Nile was a powerful testament to their success, but the journey was far from over.

They had awakened the Guardians, but now they needed to confront the larger challenge: the global threats to the oceans and rivers, and to unite humanity in the cause of conservation.

The next step was clear—Fin Man and the Guardians had to spread the message of their mission to every corner of the globe, inspiring people to take action and protect the waters that sustained life.

They needed to harness the power of their combined strengths to fight against the forces that sought to exploit and destroy the natural world.

Their first task was to return to the heart of the ocean, to the place where it all began—the site of the original call that had brought them together.

They gathered once more at the underwater sanctuary where the Heart of the Sea pulsed with its gentle, rhythmic beat.

The ocean around them was calm and clear, the beauty of the underwater world a stark contrast to the challenges they faced.

And as the Guardians assembled, Fin Man felt a deep sense of gratitude for their partnership and their shared commitment to the cause. With each Guardian bringing something unique to the table:

Marra with her life-giving powers, Aegir with his profound wisdom of the depths, and

Anuket with her connection to the flow of rivers and freshwater. Coralyth, with her wisdom of the reefs, and Callista, with her love for humanity and willingness to embrace land dwellers.

"It's time to take the next step," Fin Man said, his voice filled with determination.

"We've restored the balance in specific areas, but we need to reach out to the world, to make people understand the urgency of this mission and inspire them to take action."

Marra, her presence radiant with life, nodded in agreement.

"The power of the Guardians can be a beacon of hope, but it's the collective action of humanity that will make the difference.

We need to show them what's at stake and how they can be a part of the solution."

Aegir, his massive form casting a shadow over the ocean floor, spoke with a deep, resonant voice.

"The ocean's voice must be heard. We must use our powers to amplify it, to reach those who can make change."

Anuket, her form flowing like liquid gold, added, "We must also focus on the source of the problem—those who exploit and harm the waters.

We need to implement a better plan and address both the symptoms and the causes, to ensure that our efforts lead to lasting change."

Aegir, with great knowledge of the depths, opened the plan discussion by speaking of the primary issues:

"Rising temperatures are altering entire marine ecosystems and destabilizing the climate system. We must focus on climate change. ocean warming, acidification, and deoxygenation, which threaten coral reefs, fisheries, and global weather patterns."

Then he added, "We've already begun to address plastics, but the work must continue because plastic pollution is an enormous issue. It harms wildlife and disrupts ecosystems. Plastics also break down into microplastics that infiltrate the food chain."

Anuket spoke next, "It is essential to make humanity aware of the dangers of overfishing and illegal fishing too. The laws are in place to protect the ocean. And unsustainable fishing practices are pushing many species toward collapse while destabilizing food webs."

Callista added, "Coastal development, dredging, bottom trawling, and industrial activity damage coral reefs, mangroves, seagrass beds, and deep-sea habitats. So we must navigate how to make humanity aware of the importance of confronting this habitat destruction."

Coralyth chimed in, "Runoff from agriculture, sewage, and industry contributes to dead zones and toxic algae blooms. The chemical and nutrient pollution is harming marine life and human health."

Marra then excitedly said, "Catastrophic oil spills and industrial accidents —like Deepwater Horizon—cause long-lasting damage to marine ecosystems and coastal communities. We must continue in this work of confronting oil and gas companies, who are at the source of these issues. We must bring to their knowledge the importance of safety and clean water before profits."

Fin Man said, "Powerful economic interests continue to drive marine destruction. We must make humanity aware of the triple planetary crisis that ensues. Climate change, biodiversity loss, and pollution are converging to create a global emergency for the ocean."

So the Guardians forged a plan and agreed to begin. They would use their powers to create a series of influential symbolic actions that would capture the world's attention and convey the importance of water conservation.

They would strive to work with scientists, activists, and leaders to amplify their message and inspire global action. Fin Man would be the one to bring the ideas to them into focus.

They would need to have the first of these actions be to create a stunning display of the ocean's beauty and power.

Coralyth the Radiant would use her life-giving abilities to rejuvenate a series of coral reefs around the world, creating vibrant underwater gardens that potently serve as living examples of the ocean's potential for recovery.

These reefs will be a symbol of hope, showing that with care and action, the ocean can heal.

And Aegir and Fin Man will collaborate with oceanographers to map and protect the deepest parts of the ocean, ensuring that these critical areas remain safe from exploitation and harm. The work highlights the importance of preserving the ocean's mysteries and the ecosystems that thrive in the depths.

Anuket planned to focus on the river systems around the globe. Working with conservationists to restore and protect the world's freshwater sources.

The efforts would include cleaning polluted rivers, advocating for sustainable water management, and raising awareness about the vital role of freshwater in the health of the planet.

All together, the Guardians' plan included launching a global campaign to clean up the oceans and unite people in the cause of water conservation.

Utilizing their combined influence, they would rally support from grassroots movements to international agreements. The idea would be to create a wave of change that would ripple through every corner of the world.

Fin Man said, "The media is essential for our campaign. We can begin with a breathtaking underwater broadcast, showcasing the newly restored coral reefs and the vibrant marine life that thrives within them.

This broadcast will be transmitted through every major channel Worldwide and will undoubtedly captivate audiences around the globe. People are sure to be awed by the beauty of the ocean and moved by the message of hope and urgency."

Behind the scenes, they would participate in revealing ancient wisdom at environmental forums while meeting with world leaders.

Fin Man and the Guardians believed that each with their unique efforts, as they gained momentum, could achieve great progress and great things. Their presence and message would surely resonate with people everywhere, sparking a global conservation movement.

The goal is to see communities begin to act. Organizing clean-up efforts for their local rivers and beaches, advocating for policies to protect water sources, and educating others about the importance of sustainable water use.

The Guardians were ready and willing, knowing that they would inspire a new generation of stewards, committed to safeguarding the planet's precious resources.

Fin Man understood that the impact of their work could be profound. With the guidance of the Heart of the Sea, he believed the ocean's ecosystems could heal, rivers could run clearer, and the planet's health could begin to rebound.

His calling felt unmistakable now, and he sensed that the world was finally ready to take a meaningful step toward restoring balance. The

Guardians would be essential to transformation. Each one was a force the planet desperately needed.

Their ideas were gathering strength, between them, like a current that could not be stopped. Momentum seemed to swell around their mission, growing with every passing day.

In the heart of the underwater sanctuary, Fin Man and the Guardians continued to assemble together to chart their next steps.

The Heart of the Sea continued pulsing in Fan Man's pocket with a steady, contented beat, reflecting the positive changes that had been set in motion.

"This is just the beginning," Fin Man said, his voice filled with gratitude and hope.

"We've made a difference, but there's still much work to be done. The world must continue to value and protect its waters. We must not lose sight of our purpose to ensure that the balance we've restored is maintained."

Marra, her presence glowing with life, nodded.

"The ocean's voice has been heard, but it must remain strong. We must continue to inspire, to lead, and to protect the waters that sustain us all."

Aegir, his form merging with the depths, added;

"The mysteries of the ocean are vast, and the work of safeguarding them is never-ending. But together, we can ensure that the ocean remains a source of wonder and life."

Anuket, her flowing form shimmering in the water, concluded;

"The rivers and oceans are the veins of our planet, and their health is essential to the well-being of all living things. We must remain vigilant, dedicated, and united in our efforts."

The Turning Tide

As they looked out over the ocean, Fin Man felt a deep sense of fulfillment.

The journey had been long and challenging, but it had also been incredibly rewarding.

The future of the world's waters had never looked brighter. With the Guardians awakened, people everywhere were beginning to understand the true importance of protecting and conserving water. A global movement was taking shape—one powerful enough to spark lasting change.

Fin Man and the Guardians had made their mark, and their efforts would echo through generations. The ocean's voice now rose with renewed strength, and the rivers moved with a freer, clearer pulse. Slowly but unmistakably, the balance of the waters was being restored.

Each felt a sense of peace and accomplishment, for the time being, but was also painfully aware that their mission was far from over.

The ocean world will need ongoing care and vigilance. And with everyone included, humanity and the power of the Guardians the waters can remain a source of life, beauty, and hope.

As the sun set over the ocean, Fin Man and the Guardians stood together, ready to face whatever challenges lay ahead. Their journey had been a testament to the power of unity, the strength of nature, and the enduring spirit of the sea.

This adventure of Fin Man and the Guardians was only the beginning—a story of hope, transformation, and the boundless possibilities rising from the heart of the ocean.

The waters had awakened, the world had begun to listen, and a new tide of change was gathering strength. And though this chapter had come to a close, the currents whispered of journeys yet to come.